D is for Duck Calls

Miss Kay Robertson

Illustrated by Sydney Hanson

Simon & Schuster Books for Young Readers

New York   London   Toronto   Sydney   New Delhi

Cowritten by Chrys Howard

SIMON & SCHUSTER BOOKS FOR YOUNG READERS
An imprint of Simon & Schuster Children's Publishing Division
1230 Avenue of the Americas, New York, New York 10020

SIMON & SCHUSTER BOOKS FOR YOUNG READERS is a trademark of Simon & Schuster, Inc.
For information about special discounts for bulk purchases, please contact Simon & Schuster
Special Sales at 1-866-506-1949 or business@simonandschuster.com.
The Simon & Schuster Speakers Bureau can bring authors to your live event.
For more information or to book an event, contact the Simon & Schuster Speakers Bureau
at 1-866-248-3049 or visit our website at www.simonspeakers.com.
The text for this book is set in Chaloops Decaf.
The illustrations for this book are rendered in pencil, gouache, and digital media.
Manufactured in the United States of America
0414 PCR
2 4 6 8 10 9 7 5 3 1
Library of Congress Cataloging-in-Publication Data
Robertson, Kay, 1946–
D is for duck calls / Kay Robertson ; illustrated by Sydney Hanson. — First edition.
pages cm
Summary: "This picture book takes readers from A to Z through the world of the Duck
Commander family"— Provided by publisher.
ISBN 978-1-4814-1819-5 (hardback) — ISBN 978-1-4814-1820-1 (ebook)
I. Hanson, Sydney, illustrator. II. Duck dynasty (Television program) III. Title.
PZ8.3.R5465Daai 2014
[E]—dc23
2014001041

To all my grandchildren—
Alex, Anna, Reed, Rebecca, John Luke, Sadie, Cole,
Will, Bella, Lily, Mia, Merritt, Priscilla, River—
and my great-grandchildren—
Carley, Bailey, and Corban.
One of the greatest joys in my life
has been reading to you.
You have allowed me to keep my
house full of children's books and,
in that way, I still get to be a child.

A is for America,
land of the free.
Put your hand to your heart
and say the pledge with me.

B is for Bobo.
He's one of my dogs.
He runs after cars
and chases the frogs!

C is for Christmas,
the best time of year.
Jase hangs the lights,
and Phil cooks the deer.

D is for duck calls,
Phil's famous invention.
He blows from the duck blind,
and ducks pay attention.

E is for eggnog,
a sweet Christmas treat.
Perfect for drinking
with crawfish pie to eat!

F is for family.
It's time for a pic.
Wait! You're not our family!
Is this just a trick?

G is for grandkids,
and I have a bunch—
seventeen and counting.
I love them so much!

H is for HEY.
It's Si's favorite word.
"Hey, Jack!" he might say
to a low-flying bird.

I is for iced tea,
sweet or unsweet.
Breakfast, lunch, or supper,
it's a great Southern treat!

J is for Jase,
our second-born son.
We had Alan and Willie,
and with Jep, WE WERE DONE!

K is for kitchen.
I'll cook what you wish—
maybe warm biscuits
or mustard-fried fish?

L is for Louisiana.
It's got Cajun flair;
magnolias and honeysuckle
sweeten the air.

Louisiana

M is for Miss Kay.
I'm the family queen!
I play it in real life
and on the small screen.

N is for neighbors.
We hold them so dear.
We love that our family
lives oh so near.

O is for opossum.
They come out at night.
Watch when you're driving;
they love the bright light!

P is for Papaw Phil,
man of my dreams.
He hunts and he fishes
on rivers and streams.

Q is for QUACK,
the sound of a duck.
But ducks don't really quack,
just like chickens don't cluck!

R is for Robertson,
our family name.
Can you list us all?
We'll make it a game.

S is for squirrel.
Si tells us to try
to spell the word "squirrel"
without using S I.

T is for TV.
It made ME a STAR.
Who would have thought?
This is really bizarre!

U is for uncle.
Do you have one too?
An uncle whose stories
are 95 percent true?

V is for vacation.
The beach is such fun.
Our family just loves
to relax in the sun!

W is for Willie,
the swamp's business guru.
He works in his office
or on the bayou!

X is for XOXO,
a greeting from above—
hugs and kisses from Heaven
as God sends His love.

Y is for yuppies.
Phil likes to joke
that his redneck sons
are now city folk!

Z is for zoo,
where the wild things play—
or just like my house
when my grandkids come stay!